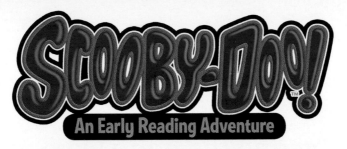

LIGHTS OUT AT THE BALL GAME

By Ellen Guidone
Illustrated by Duendes del Sur

ABDOPUBLISHING.COM

Reinforced library bound edition published in 2017 by Spotlight, a division of ABDO. PO Box 398166, Minneapolis, Minnesota 55439. Spotlight produces high-quality reinforced library bound editions for schools and libraries. Published by agreement with Warner Bros. Entertainment Inc.

Printed in the United States of America, North Mankato, Minnesota.
042016   092016

THIS BOOK CONTAINS
RECYCLED MATERIALS

PUBLISHER'S CATALOGING IN PUBLICATION DATA

Names: Guidone, Ellen, author. | Duendes del Sur, illustrator.
Title: Scooby-Doo in lights out at the ball game / by Ellen Guidone ; illustrated by Duendes del Sur.
Description: Minneapolis, MN : Spotlight, [2017] | Series: Scooby-Doo early reading adventures
Summary: Scooby and the gang are at a baseball game. When the lights go out and the coach and mascot disappear, it's up to the Mystery Inc. gang to solve the mystery and save the game.
Identifiers: LCCN 2016930656 | ISBN 9781614794752 (lib. bdg.)
Subjects: LCSH: Scooby-Doo (Fictitious character)--Juvenile fiction. | Dogs--Juvenile fiction. | Baseball--Juvenile fiction. | Ghosts--Juvenile fiction. | Mystery and detective stories--Juvenile fiction. | Adventure and adventurers--Juvenile fiction.
Classification: DDC [Fic]--dc23
LC record available at http://lccn.loc.gov/2016930656

Spotlight
A Division of ABDO
abdopublishing.com

Scooby and the gang were at a baseball game.

They were excited to watch their favorite team, the Bulldogs, play the Wildcats.

"This is going to be a great game!" Fred said.

"Like, especially with all these snacks," said Shaggy.

"Reah!" added Scooby.

Fred, Velma and Daphne settled in for the game.

"Go Bulldogs!" cheered Fred.

Scooby and Shaggy played a game of their own.

Shaggy threw peanuts into the air and Scooby caught them in his mouth.

"This is the best game ever!" said Shaggy.

Suddenly, all the lights went out.
The stadium was pitch-black.
Fred turned on his flashlight, and
Scooby and Shaggy made shadow
puppets on the stadium wall.
Then Fred overheard two players
talking about their coach and the
team's bulldog, Lucky.
"The coach is missing," said one
player to the other.
"So is our pal Lucky. What are
we going to do without our coach
and mascot?"

"Oh no! The Bulldogs can't play without their coach or their mascot," Fred said to the gang.

"I wonder where they are," said Velma.

"I hope they're not in trouble," said Daphne.

"Like, I hope they weren't taken by a ghost," said Shaggy.

"Let's look for clues," said Fred.

"Like, we can't look for clues on an empty stomach," said Shaggy.

"Reah!" said Scooby.

"Scoob, you search for clues by the popcorn and I'll check out the hot dogs," said Shaggy.

"Rokay!" said Scooby.

Shaggy picked out a hot dog and Scooby munched on popcorn.

They did not find any clues at the snack bar, only pretzels, peanuts, hot dogs, popcorn and soda.

Next, Scooby and Shaggy looked for clues in the gift shop.

Shaggy picked up a baseball and a glove.

Scooby picked up a bat.

"Hey Scoob, batter up!" Shaggy said.

Shaggy pitched the ball to Scooby.

Scooby swung the bat and drove the ball out of the room.

Scooby took off after the ball.
It rolled into a room at the end
of the hall.
It was the Bulldogs' locker room.
The gang was already there,
investigating a loud noise
coming from the closet.

Everyone heard banging, howling and scratching noises coming from the closet.

"It's the ghost!" cried Shaggy.

"I have an idea," Velma said. "Scooby, would you open that door?" she asked.

"Ro way!" said Scooby.

"Would you do it for a Scooby-Snack?" she asked.

"Rokay!" Scooby said.

Scooby opened the closet and found a big surprise.

Lucky, the Bulldogs' mascot, and Whiskers, the Wildcats' mascot, burst out of the closet.

"Guess we know who was doing all the howling and scratching," Velma said.

"Then who was banging?" Shaggy asked. "Was it a ghost?"

"Nope. That was me," said the Bulldogs' coach, stepping through the door.

"I came here to fix the lights and Lucky and Whiskers chased me into the closet. It was so dark I couldn't find the light switch."

"It's a good thing we found you," Fred said.

"It sure is," said the coach. "Thanks to you, we can continue the game."

"Scooby, you saved the baseball game!" said Daphne.

Scooby picked up a bat and swung it like a pro.

"Scoob's ready to play too," said Shaggy.

"You can be our next hitter," said the coach.

"Scooby-Dooby-Doo!" Scooby barked.

The End